Once upon a time there was a very old man and a very old woman.

They lived
in a nice, clean
house, which had
flowers all around it,
except where the door was.

But they were so very lonely.

"If only we had a cat!" sighed the very old woman.

"A cat?" asked the very old man.

"Yes, a sweet, little, fluffy cat," said the very old woman.

"I will get you a cat, my dear," said the very old man.

And he set out over the hills to look for one.

He climbed over the sunny hills.

He trudged through the cool valleys.

He walked a long, long time.
At last, he came to a hill
where …

Cats here, cats there.
Cats and kittens, everywhere.

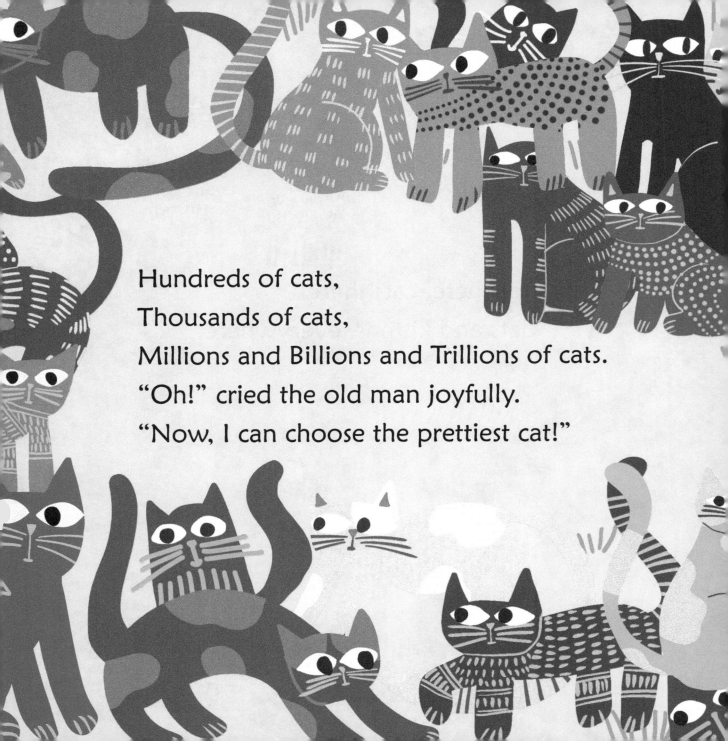

Hundreds of cats,
Thousands of cats,
Millions and Billions and Trillions of cats.
"Oh!" cried the old man joyfully.
"Now, I can choose the prettiest cat!"

But just as he was
about to leave ...

and before he knew it, he had chosen them all.

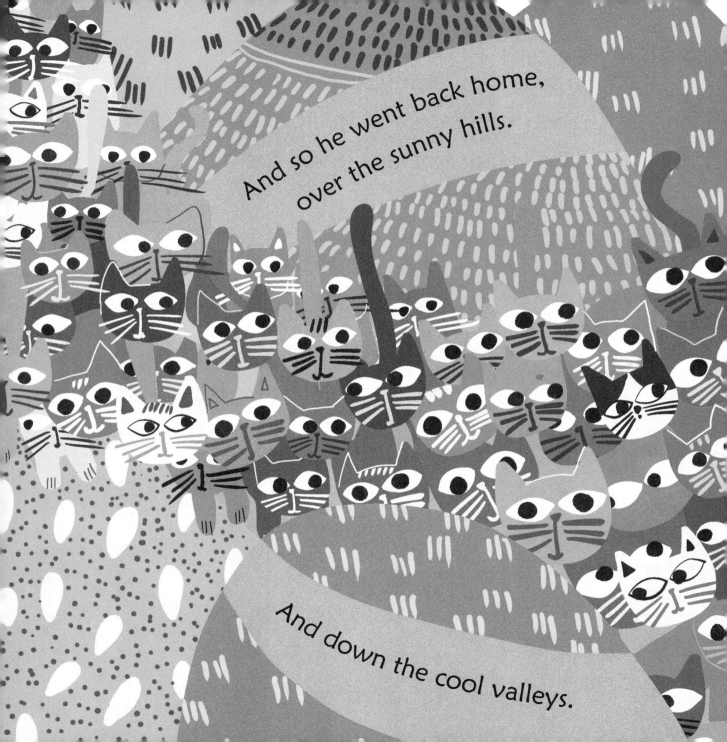

And so he went back home, over the sunny hills.

And down the cool valleys.

It was very funny to see those hundreds and thousands and millions and billions and trillions of cats following him.

They came to a pond.

"Mew, mew! We are thirsty!"
cried the Hundreds of cats,
Thousands of cats, the Millions
and Billions and Trillions of cats.

Each cat took a sip of water,
and the pond was gone!

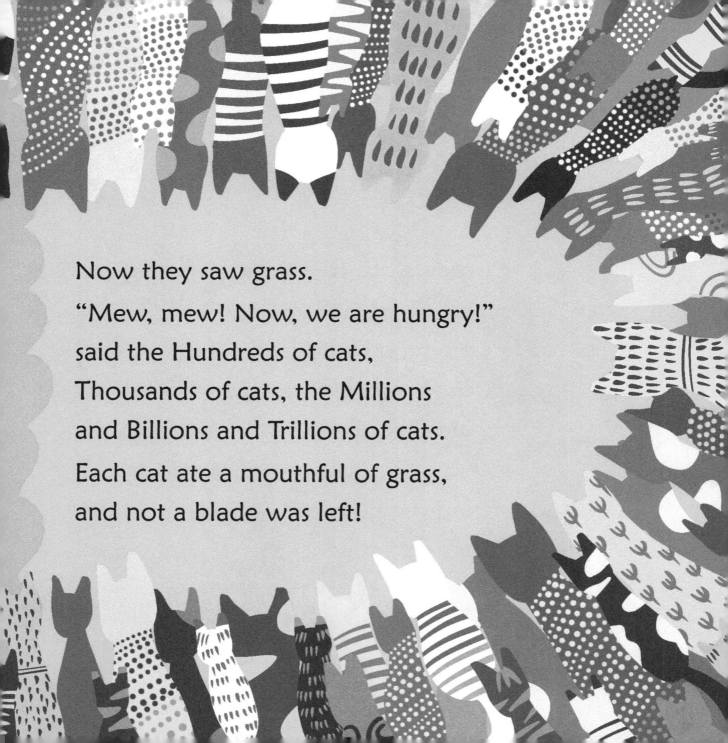

Now they saw grass.

"Mew, mew! Now, we are hungry!"
said the Hundreds of cats,
Thousands of cats, the Millions
and Billions and Trillions of cats.

Each cat ate a mouthful of grass,
and not a blade was left!

Pretty soon the very old woman saw them coming.
"My dear!" she cried, "What are you doing?
I asked for one little cat, and what do I see?"

"Cats here, Cats there,
Cats and kittens everywhere,
Hundreds of cats,

Thousands of cats,
The Millions and Billions of cats."

"But we can never feed them all," said the very old woman. She thought for a while and then she said, "I know! I will let the cats decide which one we should keep."

"Oh yes," said the very old man, and he called to the cats ...

"No, I am!" "I am the prettiest!" cried hundreds and thousands and the millions and billions and trillions of voices, for each cat thought itself the prettiest. And they began to quarrel. They bit and scratched and clawed each other, and made such a great noise.

But after a while the noise stopped, and the very old man and the very old woman peeped out of the window to see what had happened.

They could not see
a single cat!

"But look!" said the very old man.
In a bunch of high grass sat one little frightened kitten.
"Poor little kitty," said the very old woman.
"Dear little kitty," said the very old man,
"Why, what happened to you?"

"Oh, I'm just a very ordinary little cat," said the kitten. "So when you asked who was the prettiest, I didn't say anything. So nobody bothered about me."

They took the kitten into the house, where
the very old woman gave it a warm bath and
brushed its fur until it was soft and shiny.

Every day they gave it plenty of milk —
and soon it grew nice and plump.

"And it is a very pretty cat, after all!" said the very old woman.

"It is the most beautiful cat in the whole world," said the very old man. "I ought to know, for I've seen —

Hundreds of cats. Thousands of cats. Millions and Billions and Trillions of cats — and not one was as pretty as this one."

Think

Why do you think the old man and woman felt lonely? Why do you think people feel lonely?

Ask

How would a cat help the old woman and man feel less lonely? What can people do to feel less lonely?

Discuss

Why did the old couple find the little kitten the prettiest?

Achieve

Similar to the hills, the
streets that we walk on
every day have many, many
stray animals.

Can you help the street
animals near your neighbourhood
find a shelter or a home?
Give them some food
that you can spare.
Leave out some water in big clay
bowls for stray cats,
dogs and birds.

Act

Imagine what happened
after the old man and
woman started taking
care of the kitten.
Write a story of what
happens next.

Wanda Gág was an American artist, author, translator, illustrator, and a distinguished print-maker. Best known for "Millions of Cats", the oldest American picture book still in print, she had won many international recognitions and awards including the Newbery Honors and the Caldecott Honors.

Boski Jain is a visual designer and illustrator with a special fondness for drawing animals. She enjoys taking inspiration from Indian folk art while creating characters and patterns for her work. Born and brought up in Bhopal, she currently lives in Bangalore.

KATHA

Copyright © Katha, 2020

Text copyright © Wanda Gag, 1928

Illustration copyright © Boski Jain, 2020

All rights reserved. No part of this book may be reproduced or utilized in any form without the prior written permission of the publisher.

Printed in New Delhi

ISBN 978-93-88284-88-2

Our Mission: Every child reading well for fun and meaning!

KATHA is a registered nonprofit organization started in 1988. We work in the literacy to literature continuum. Devoted to enhancing the joys of reading amongst children and adults, we work with more than 1,00,000 children in poverty, to bring them to grade-level reading through quality books and interventions.

A3, Sarvodaya Enclave, Sri Aurobindo Marg, New Delhi 110 017

Phone: 4141 6600 . 4182 9998 . 2652 1752

E-mail: marketing@katha.org, Website: www.katha.org, www.books.katha.org

First published by G.P. Putnam's Sons-Penguin Books USA ("Millions of Cats"), 1928

Ten per cent of sales proceeds from this book will support the quality education of children studying in Katha schools.
Katha regularly plants trees to replace the wood used in the making of its books.

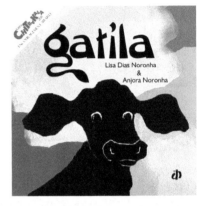

PAINT LIKE FRANZ MARC
Geeta Dharmarajan
Art by Franz Marc

A book meant for colourful hearts and creative minds! Gently guides children to engage with each of German painter Franz Marc's works through a simple but reflective questions. This book will encourage children and adults alike to don the artist's cap.

TIGERS FOREVER!
Ruskin Bond
Art by David Stribbling

Let's protect and save our tiger friends!

GATILA
Lisa Dias Noronha &
Anjora Noronha

Gatila does not think she is a pretty cow. But she has a solution. And so, quietly in the night, plop goes her tail in the paint cans.

What happens next? Find out in multicolour!

FOR THE LOVE OF A CAT
Rosalind Wilson | Art by Wen Hsu

A painter loves his cat as much as he loves painting. But when the starving artist is commissioned to paint a picture of the Buddha, he must choose between his art and his pet …

A colourful read that introduces children to the common thread of feelings running through all living things.

CPSIA information can be obtained
at www.ICGtesting.com
Printed in the USA
LVHW061536270223
740495LV00009B/754

9 789388 284882